THE HOUSE OF JOYFUL LIVING

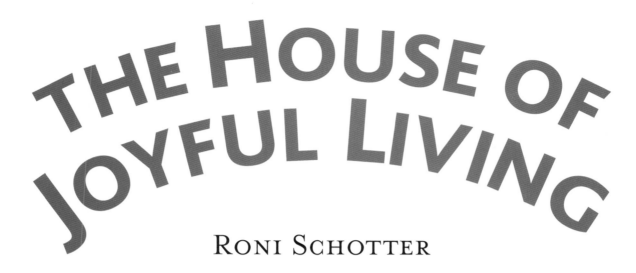

RONI SCHOTTER

PICTURES BY TERRY WIDENER

MELANIE KROUPA BOOKS
Farrar, Straus and Giroux / New York

For Ellen Braune and Toby and Bruce Dale, who make this world a House of Joyful Living.
For Ilsa, Nathan and Jordan Halpern, and Susan Mende, in loving memory of Curly and Tuz Mende
and all the good people of the House of Joyful Living
—R.S.

For LSW (30)
—T.W.

Text copyright © 2008 by Roni Schotter
Pictures copyright © 2008 by Terry Widener
Distributed in Canada by Douglas & McIntyre Ltd.
Color separations by Chroma Graphics PTE Ltd.
Printed and bound in China by South China Printing Co. Ltd.
Designed by Jay Colvin
First edition, 2008
1 3 5 7 9 10 8 6 4 2

www.fsgkidsbooks.com

Library of Congress Cataloging-in-Publication Data
Schotter, Roni.
    The House of Joyful Living / Roni Schotter ; pictures by Terry Widener.— 1st ed.
        p. cm.
    Summary: A young girl loves her busy, crowded apartment building where neighbors enjoy
spending time together in the roof garden, but she becomes very jealous when the new baby
her mother is expecting takes attention away from herself.
    ISBN-13: 978-0-374-33429-1
    ISBN-10: 0-374-33429-3
    [1. Apartment houses—Fiction. 2. Neighborliness—Fiction. 3. Jealousy—Fiction.
4. Family life—New York (State)—New York—Fiction. 5. New York (N.Y.)—Fiction.]
    I. Widener, Terry, ill. II. Title.

PZ7.S3765Hou 2008
[E]—dc22

                                                                        2007005100

The brick was crumbling. The paint was peeling. But we called it "the House of Joyful Living." Long ago, when I was small and round and had cabbage-curly hair, I lived there.

Whenever we could, we climbed the stairs to the roof of the House of Joyful Living. Mama climbed slowly. Her belly was heavy. Something was growing inside.

High on the roof was a garden with flowers, potted trees, stone sculptures, a goldfish pond, and a hawk's-eye view of the buildings around us, even the Empire State Building. With a mama and papa all to myself, it seemed I lived on top of the world—in paradise.

On the roof, everyone gathered, to read, to weed, to chat—great, good grownups with great, good names: Curly and Touz, Frenchie and Horty, Dick and Gene-vieve. Many grownups, a bulldog named Nicky, but *only one child*—me!

Always there was music. It came through Mama's radio from other great, good grownups with great, good names—Mendelssohn, Mozart, and Bach. Sometimes we hummed. Often we danced. *Always* I smiled. High above the roof of the House of Joyful Living, the clouds paused to gather and watch. The pigeons leaned in to listen.

On Sundays, Papa and Dick brought breakfast for anyone who wanted—slices of challah bread, platters of pickled herring, tuna salad with eggs and onions chopped right in, and *a special plate*—just for *me*! Mama held me close in her lap, her long lashes tickling my cheek, and told me stories about the work she and Papa, Dick and Gene, Curly and Touz had done during the week to help people, people not as lucky as we were, people with no challah, herring, or Roof Garden.

Then Frenchie, with Horty as his assistant, snipped and folded the Sunday comics into strange birds with wings that flapped when you pulled on them. "*Wah-zoh*," he called the birds, so I could learn to say their name the way people did in the faraway place where he was born, the place he called "*Pa-ree*."

At last it was *my* turn! I showed my signs—the pictures I'd drawn that Papa helped me add words to— to remind people, rich and poor, of what he and Mama always told me was important, that everyone should "share with one another and *never* be selfish or greedy." When I finished, Curly and Touz gave me hugs.

One Sunday—*chip, chip, ring*—I hear sounds from Behind-the-Storage-Shed. Mr. Carriero, from Down-the-Block, is carving. Before he lived Down-the-Block, he was a stonemason in a faraway place he called Catania, in a country he called "*EE-taly*." It was he who made the statues and sculptures for our Roof Garden. Now he is working on something new, something *mysterious*, something covered in cloth . . .

"What *is* it?" I ask.

"*S'a* secret surprise," he answers, "for to give to someone *special*."

Someone special? It *must*, of course, be *me*! "Is it ready?" I ask.

"No' yet," he answers. "Ready soon—for Roof Party."

Roof Party, I realize, it's coming!

Once a summer in the House of Joyful Living, it was "Roof Party!" Everyone invited *everyone* to our roof— Mrs. Ling, who helped with our garden; Miss Farrell, the Fish Lady, who knew everything about goldfish; even people the grownups knew, who I didn't know. To be ready, we sweep and scrub and paint. We hang lanterns and lots of lights. Then, of course, we cook!

In our tiny kitchen, we make a treat Papa's grandma cooked years ago in *her* tiny kitchen, far away in a land called Russia. "Potato pockets!" I call them, but their real name is *pirogen*. Papa says Great-grandma's recipe starts with kisses. After that, we fry onions, mash potatoes, and cover them in dough. Soon our kitchen smells of love and long ago.

Upstairs in Curly and Touz's apartment, they roast vegetables. Down in Dick and Gene's, they chop onions for their tuna. Over at Frenchie and Horty's, they cook the *wah-zoh* Frenchie calls *pooh-lay* but we call chicken. In other apartments, they bake breads and cookies and cakes. The smoke and smells waft and weave their way through the hallways of the House of Joyful Living, until they reach the roof and surround it in a halo.

"Time to deliver the goods!" Papa says when we finish our frying. Mama carries our platter of *pirogen*, resting it on her belly that is growing bigger every month. Mama says a *baby* is growing inside her, but I don't like to think about that, so I say it is too many *pirogen*! Papa carries *me*, high on his shoulders, and I carry my signs! Up to the roof of the House of Joyful Living we go. "Come out! Come out!" I call to everyone in the Building. Dick wheels my old baby carriage, filled now with everyone's food. Nicky hurries hungrily along.

On the roof, our special guests are waiting—Mr. Carriero, of course; Mrs. Ling and the Little Lings from the Building-Next-Door; Miss Farrell, the Fish Lady; and some of the people the grownups help during the week.

Mrs. Ling wears her gardener's apron with pockets filled with seeds for our garden. Always she brings flowers. "You share bread, so I share roses. Bread and roses," she says. "To be happy, people need both!"

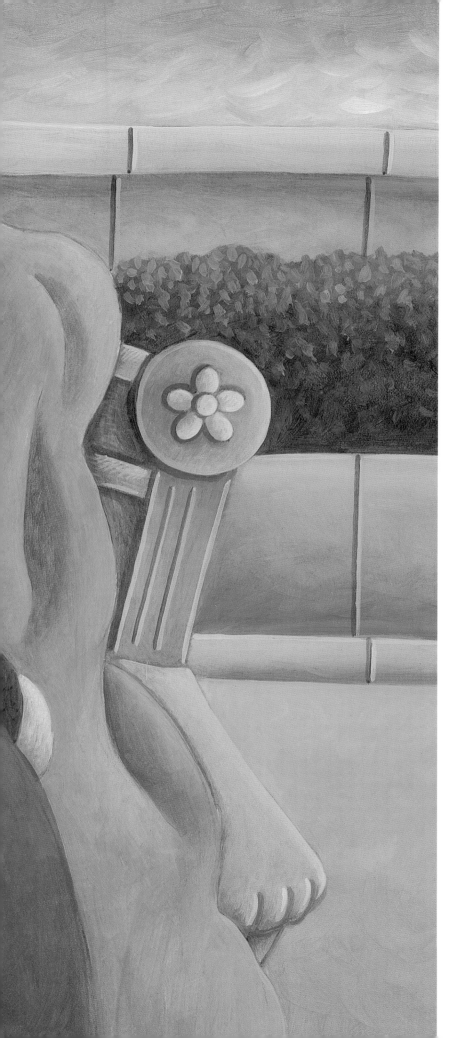

Mr. Carriero brings his hammer and chisel—his hammer and chisel and the secret surprise!

"Today, I have a special announce," he says. "I *make-a* a gift! Very soon comes the new baby, *so*," he says, lifting the cloth, "I *carve-a* you, Mrs. Goldberg, a special chair, *just-a* for you and the baby, for to sit upon, *together*. If a boy, I carve a *putto* on the back; if a girl, a *putta*. Either way, will be an *angel*, like this one you already have," he says, cupping my face in his hand.

I pull my face away. I don't *feel* like an angel! I run as far away as I can, to the goldfish pond. Nicky runs after me. No one else notices. They are busy hugging Mama, patting her belly—her belly full-of-*baby*! Soon Mama will be busy, too—busy with the baby—too busy for me.

In the rippling water of the goldfish pond I see a sad and angry face. I watch the goldfish flip their floppy fantails and pout their puffy lips, the same way I pout mine.

I think about Gene and Dick and my special plate. About Curly and Touz and their hugs. About Frenchie and Horty and the *wah-zoh*. Most of all, I think about Mama and Papa and the new baby.

Soon Mama will sit with it in Mr. Carriero's special chair. She will hold it in her lap and tickle its cheeks with her lashes. Papa will carry it high on his shoulders. Everyone in the House of Joyful Living will pay attention to the baby and forget about me. Soon it won't feel like a House of Joyful Living anymore.

Nicky nuzzles me. His thirsty tongue laps tears from my wet face. I see my signs—my signs about sharing. I don't care what Mama and Papa have taught me. I *don't* want to share *anything*—not even Nicky! I want everything for myself.

Then there are arms—Mama's. And there is Mr. Carriero, smiling sadly, carrying his chair over. Mama sits me, finds a way to fit me, into her lumpy, very *bumpy* lap. She gives me butterfly kisses with her lashes, and I give them back. The baby is moving. "What's it *doing* in there?" I ask.

"*Feels* like it's dancing, but, *ouch*, I'm afraid it hasn't much room."

"Well, there *isn't* any room *here*—not in your lap! It's *full* . . . What's it like *inside*?"

"Crowded," Mama says, "but cozy and warm, full of food and love."

"Like the House of Joyful Living," I say, "but without all the people. Mama, your *belly* is a house of joyful living! Maybe the baby won't *want* to come out . . ."

Mama laughs and twirls my cabbage curls. "It will want to meet you, and Papa, and Curly and Touz and Dick and Gene and everyone in *our* House of Joyful Living."

I look around. Miss Farrell is feeding our fish. Frenchie is winking and working on a paper animal for me. Mrs. Ling is pruning our yew bush. Mr. Carriero is fixing the smile on one of his statues. Gene and Dick are passing out *pirogen*. Curly has turned on the music—Mozart.

Now Papa is here. Together, he and Mama hold me, find a way to fold me into their arms, and suddenly I am the center of the warmest and best of *all* houses. The lump that is the baby bumps me. I think it is jealous.

Papa lifts me high onto his shoulders. "Look out there . . ." he says.

I see the Statue of Liberty raising her arm as if she is waving to me. I see a river with a bridge like a giant spiderweb across it. On the other side is the faraway place they call Brooklyn. Beyond Brooklyn is the ocean. Beyond that, beckoning, is the rest of the world . . .